James Jeffrey Roche

Ballads of Blue Water

And Other Poems

James Jeffrey Roche

Ballads of Blue Water
And Other Poems

ISBN/EAN: 9783744778114

Printed in Europe, USA, Canada, Australia, Japan

Cover: Foto ©Andreas Hilbeck / pixelio.de

More available books at **www.hansebooks.com**

BALLADS OF BLUE WATER
AND OTHER POEMS

BY

JAMES JEFFREY ROCHE

BOSTON AND NEW YORK
HOUGHTON, MIFFLIN AND COMPANY
The Riverside Press, Cambridge
1895

The Riverside Press, Cambridge, Mass., U. S. A.
Electrotyped and Printed by H. O. Houghton & Co.

DEDICATION

TO MY CANOE, "WANDA"

*Of distant deeds sing I who ne'er
Did anything, went anywhere;*

*Of storm and battle on the blue —
Whose total fleet is one canoe.*

*I might, had Fortune so inclined,
Have fought, and left my shield behind!*

*Let him who takes his armor off
Boast if he will; and should he scoff*

*At us who never put it on,
Still may we praise the heroes gone,*

*And rest content that we have known
Some joys that go with peace alone.*

*The bark that carried Cæsar's fate
Bore never such a precious freight*

*As thou didst bear, one day, when She
Sang, not of war, for thee and me.*

CONTENTS

The author acknowledges his thanks to The Century Company,
"The Atlantic Monthly," Messrs. Charles Scribner's Sons, and
Messrs. Harper and Brothers for permission to republish several
poems in this collection.

BALLADS OF BLUE WATER AND OTHER POEMS

THE FIGHT OF THE "ARMSTRONG" PRIVATEER

TELL the story to your sons
    Of the gallant days of yore,
  When the brig of seven guns
    Fought the fleet of seven score,
From the set of sun till morn, through the long
September night —
Ninety men against two thousand, and the ninety
won the fight
    In the harbor of Fayal the Azore.

Three lofty British ships came a-sailing to Fayal :
One was a line-of-battle ship, and two were frigates
    tall ;
Nelson's valiant men of war, brave as Britons ever
    are,
Manned the guns they served so well at Aboukir
    and Trafalgar.

Lord Dundonald and his fleet at Jamaica far
    away
Waited eager for their coming, fretted sore at their
    delay.
There was loot for British valor on the Mississippi
    coast
In the beauty and the booty that the Creole cities
    boast ;
There were rebel knaves to swing, there were pris-
    oners to bring
Home in fetters to old England for the glory of the
    King !

At the setting of the sun and the ebbing of the
    tide
Came the great ships one by one, with their portals
    opened wide,
And their cannon frowning down on the castle and
    the town
And the privateer that lay close inside ;
Came the eighteen gun Carnation, and the Rota,
    forty-four,
And the triple-decked Plantagenet an admiral's
    pennon bore ;
And the privateer grew smaller as their topmasts
    towered taller,
And she bent her springs and anchored by the
    castle on the shore.

Spake the noble Portuguese to the stranger:
   "Have no fear;
They are neutral waters these, and your ship is
   sacred here
As if fifty stout armadas stood to shelter you from
   harm,
For the honor of the Briton will defend you from
   his arm."
But the privateersman said, "Well we know the
   Englishmen,
And their faith is written red in the Dartmoor
   slaughter pen.
Come what fortune God may send, we will fight
   them to the end,
And the mercy of the sharks may spare us then."

"Seize the pirate where she lies!" cried the Eng-
   lish admiral:
"If the Portuguese protect her, all the worse for
   Portugal!"
And four launches at his bidding leaped impa-
   tient for the fray,
Speeding shoreward where the Armstrong, grim
   and dark and ready, lay.
Twice she hailed and gave them warning; but the
   feeble menace scorning,
On they came in splendid silence, till a cable's
   length away —

Then the Yankee pivot spoke; Pico's thousand
echoes woke;
And four baffled, beaten launches drifted helpless
on the bay.

Then the wrath of Lloyd arose till the lion roared
again,
And he called out all his launches and he called
five hundred men;
And he gave the word " No quarter ! " and he sent
them forth to smite.
Heaven help the foe before him when the Briton
comes in might !
Heaven helped the little Armstrong in her hour of
bitter need;
God Almighty nerved the heart and guided well
the arm of Reid.

Launches to port and starboard, launches forward
and aft,
Fourteen launches together striking the little craft.
They hacked at the boarding - nettings, they
swarmed above the rail ;
But the Long Tom roared from his pivot and the
grape-shot fell like hail :
Pike and pistol and cutlass, and hearts that knew
not fear,

Bulwarks of brawn and mettle, guarded the priva-
teer.
And ever where fight was fiercest, the form of Reid
was seen ;
Ever where foes drew nearest, his quick sword fell
between.
Once in the deadly strife
The boarders' leader pressed
Forward of all the rest
Challenging life for life ;
But ere their blades had crossed,
A dying sailor tossed
His pistol to Reid, and cried,
" Now riddle the lubber's hide ! "
But the privateersman laughed, and flung the
weapon aside,
And he drove his blade to the hilt, and the foeman
gasped and died.
Then the boarders took to their launches laden
with hurt and dead,
But little with glory burdened, and out of the bat-
tle fled.

Now the tide was at flood again, and the night was
almost done,
When the sloop-of-war came up with her odds of
two to one,

And she opened fire ; but the Armstrong answered
    her, gun for gun,
And the gay Carnation wilted in half an hour of sun.

Then the Armstrong, looking seaward, saw the
    mighty seventy-four,
With her triple tier of cannon, drawing slowly to
    the shore.
And the dauntless captain said: " Take our
    wounded and our dead,
Bear them tenderly to land, for the Armstrong's
    days are o'er ;
But no foe shall tread her deck, and no flag above
    it wave —
To the ship that saved our honor we will give a
    shipman's grave."
So they did as he commanded, and they bore their
    mates to land
With the figurehead of Armstrong and the good
    sword in his hand.
Then they turned the Long Tom downward, and
    they pierced her oaken side,
And they cheered her, and they blessed her, and
    they sunk her in the tide.

Tell the story to your sons,
    When the haughty stranger boasts

Of his mighty ships and guns
And the muster of his hosts,
How the word of God was witnessed in the gallant
days of yore
When the twenty fled from one ere the rising of
the sun,
In the harbor of Fayal the Azore !

THE KEARSARGE

In the gloomy ocean bed
Dwelt a formless thing, and said,
In the dim and countless eons long ago,
   "I will build a stronghold high,
   Ocean's power to defy,
And the pride of haughty man to lay low."

Crept the minutes for the sad,
Sped the cycles for the glad,
But the march of time was neither less nor more ;
   While the formless atom died,
   Myriad millions by its side,
And above them slowly lifted Roncador.

Roncador of Caribee,
Coral dragon of the sea,
Ever sleeping with his teeth below the wave ;
   Woe to him who breaks the sleep !
   Woe to them who sail the deep !
Woe to ship and man that fear a shipman's grave !

Hither many a galleon old,
Heavy-keeled with guilty gold,
Fled before the hardy rover smiting sore ;
But the sleeper silent lay
Till the preyer and his prey
Brought their plunder and their bones to Roncador.

Be content, O conqueror !
Now our bravest ship of war,
War and tempest who had often braved before,
All her storied prowess past,
Strikes her glorious flag at last
To the formless thing that builded Roncador.

Joy in rebel Plymouth town, in the spring of sixty-
    four,
  When the Albemarle down on the Yankee frig-
      ates bore,
With the saucy Stars and Bars at her main;
  When she smote the Southfield dead, and the
      stout Miami quailed,
And the fleet in terror fled when their mighty can-
    non hailed
  Shot and shell on her iron back in vain,
Till she slowly steamed away to her berth at Ply-
    mouth pier,
  And their quick eyes saw her sway with her great
      beak out of gear,
And the color of their courage rose again.

  All the summer lay the ram,
    Like a wounded beast at bay,
  While the watchful squadron swam
    In the harbor night and day,

Till the broken beak was mended, and the weary
   vigil ended,
And her time was come again to smite and slay.

Must they die, and die in vain,
   Like a flock of shambled sheep?
Then the Yankee grit and brain
   Must be dead or gone to sleep,
And our sailors' gallant story of a hundred years
   of glory
Let us sell for a song, selling cheap!

Cushing, scarce a man in years,
   But a sailor thoroughbred,
" With a dozen volunteers
   I will sink the ram," he said.
" At the worst 't is only dying." And the old com-
   mander, sighing,
   " 'T is to save the fleet and flag — go ahead ! "
   .   .   .   .

Bright the rebel beacons blazed
   On the river left and right ;
Wide awake their sentries gazed
   Through the watches of the night ;
Sharp their challenge rang, and fiery came the
   rifle's quick inquiry,
As the little launch swung into the light.

Listening ears afar had heard ;
Ready hands to quarters sprung,
The Albemarle awoke and stirred,
And her howitzers gave tongue ;
Till the river and the shore echoed back the mighty
roar,
When the portals of her hundred-pounders swung.

Will the swordfish brave the whale,
Doubly girt with boom and chain ?
Face the shrapnel's iron hail ?
Dare the livid leaden rain ?
Ah ! that shell has done its duty ; it has spoiled
the Yankee's beauty ;
See her turn and fly with half her madmen
slain !

High the victors' taunting yell
Rings above the battle roar,
And they bid her mock farewell
As she seeks the farther shore,
Till they see her sudden swinging, crouching for
the leap and springing
Back to boom and chain and bloody fray once
more.

Now the Southron captain, stirred
   By the spirit of his race,
Stops the firing with a word,
   Bids them yield, and offers grace.
Cushing, laughing, answers, " No ! we are here to
   fight ! " and so
Swings the dread torpedo spar to its place.

Then the great ship shook and reeled,
   With a wounded, gaping side,
But her steady cannon pealed
   Ere she settled in the tide,
And the Roanoke's dull flood ran full red with
   Yankee blood,
When the fighting Albemarle sunk and died.

Woe in rebel Plymouth town when the Albemarle
   fell,
   And the saucy flag went down that had floated
   long and well,
Nevermore from her stricken deck to wave.
   For the fallen flag a sigh, for the fallen foe a
   tear !
Never shall their glory die while we hold our glory
   dear,
   And the hero's laurels live on his grave.

Link their Cooke's with Cushing's name ; proudly
  call them both our own ;
Claim their valor and their fame for America
  alone —
  Joyful mother of the bravest of the brave !

AT SEA

SHALL we, the storm-tossed sailors, weep
   For those who may not sail again ;
Or wisely envy them, and keep
   Our pity for the living men ?

Beyond the weary waste of sea,
   Beyond the wider waste of death,
I strain my gaze and cry to thee
   Whose still heart never answereth.

O brother, is thy coral bed
   So sweet thou wilt not hear my speech ?
This hand, methinks, if I were dead,
   To thy dear hand would strive to reach.

I would not, if God gave us choice
   For each to bear the other's part,
That mine should be the silent voice,
   And thine the silent, aching heart.

15

Ah, well for any voyage done,
    Whate'er its end — or port or reef ;
Better the voyage ne'er begun,
    For all ships sail the sea of Grief.

THE CONSTITUTION'S LAST FIGHT

A Yankee ship and a Yankee crew —
Constitution, where ye bound for ?
Wherever, my lad, there 's fight to be had,
Acrost the Western Ocean.

OUR captain was married in Boston town
    And sailed next day to sea ;
For all must go when the State says so ;
    Blow high, blow low, sailed we.

" Now what shall I bring for a bridal gift
    When my home-bound pennant flies ?
The rarest that be on land or sea
    It shall be my lady's prize."

"There 's never a prize on sea or land
    Could bring such joy to me
As my true love sound and homeward bound
    With a king's ship under his lee."

The Western ocean is wide and deep,
    And wild its tempests blow,

But bravely rides Old Ironsides,
  A-cruising to and fro.

We cruised to the East and we cruised to the
    North,
  And Southing far went we,
And at last off Cape de Verde we raised
  Two frigates sailing free.

Oh, God made man, and man made ships,
  But God makes very few
Like him who sailed our ship that day
  And fought her, one to two.

He gained the weather-gage of both,
  He held them both a-lee ;
And gun for gun till set of sun,
  He spoke them fair and free ;

Till the night-fog fell on spar and sail
  And ship and sea and shore,
And our only aim was the bursting flame
  And the hidden cannon's roar.

Then a lifting rift in the mist showed up
  The stout Cyane close-hauled

To swing in our wake and our quarter rake,
And a boasting Briton bawled :

" Starboard and larboard we 've got him fast
Where his heels won't carry him through :
Let him luff or wear, he 'll find us there —
Ho, Yankee, which will you do ? "

We did not luff and we did not wear,
But braced our topsails back,
Till the sternway drew us fair and true
Broadsides athwart her track.

Athwart her track and across her bows
We raked her fore and aft,
And out of the fight and into the night
Drifted the beaten craft.

The slow Levant came up too late ;
No need had we to stir.
Her decks we swept with fire and kept
The flies from troubling her.

We raked her again, and her flag came down,
The haughtiest flag that floats,
And the Limejuice dogs lay there like logs,
With never a bark in their throats.

With never a bark and never a bite,
  But only an oath, to break,
As we squared away for Praya Bay
  With our prizes in our wake.

Parole they gave and parole they broke,
  What matters the cowardly cheat,
If the captain's bride was satisfied
  With the one prize laid at her feet?

A Yankee ship and a Yankee crew —
  Constitution, where ye bound for?
Wherever the British prizes be,
  Though it 's one to two, or one to three —
Old Ironsides means Victory,
  Acrost the Western Ocean!

THREE ships of war had Preble when he left the
Naples shore,
And the knightly king of Naples lent him seven
galleys more,
And never since the Argo floated in the middle
sea
Such noble men and valiant have sailed in company
As the men who went with Preble to the siege of
Tripoli.
Stewart, Bainbridge, Hull, Decatur — how their
names ring out like gold ! —
Lawrence, Porter, Trippe, Macdonough, and a
score as true and bold ;
Every star that lights their banner tells the glory
that they won ;
But one common sailor's glory is the splendor of
the sun.

Reuben James was first to follow when Decatur
laid aboard
Of the lofty Turkish galley and in battle broke his
sword.

Then the pirate captain smote him, till his blood
    was running fast,
And they grappled and they struggled, and they
    fell beside the mast.
Close behind him Reuben battled with a dozen,
    undismayed,
Till a bullet broke his sword-arm, and he dropped
    the useless blade.
Then a swinging Turkish sabre clove his left and
    brought him low,
Like a gallant bark, dismasted, at the mercy of the
    foe.
Little mercy knows the corsair : high his blade was
    raised to slay,
When a richer prize allured him where Decatur
    struggling lay.
"Help!" the Turkish leader shouted, and his
    trusty comrade sprung,
And his scimetar like lightning o'er the Yankee
    captain swung.

Reuben James, disabled, armless, saw the sabre
    flashed on high,
Saw Decatur shrink before it, heard the pirate's
    taunting cry,
Saw, in half the time I tell it, how a sailor brave
    and true

Still might show a bloody pirate what a dying man
    can do.
Quick he struggled, stumbling, sliding in the blood
    around his feet,
As the Turk a moment waited to make vengeance
    doubly sweet.
Swift the sabre fell, but swifter bent the sailor's
    head below,
And upon his 'fenceless forehead Reuben James
    received the blow!

So was saved our brave Decatur; so the common
    sailor died;
So the love that moves the lowly lifts the great to
    fame and pride.
Yet we grudge him not his honors, for whom love
    like this had birth —
For God never ranks His sailors by the Register
    of earth!

A BUSINESS TRANSACTION

To Amsterdam and its Commodore,
   Over his pipe and his eau-de-vie,
A flibote skimming the Texel shore
   Brought serious news for the Zuyder Zee :

Forty sail of the Channel Fleet,
   With a high-born Admiral of the Blue,
Holland's bravest had come to greet
   And settle an ancient score or two.

Frugal of speech was the Commodore.
   " I will meet their wishes," he briefly said,
And straight to the offing his squadron bore,
   With a broom at the flagship's mainmast-head.

Quickly to work, in a business way,
   Went old Van Dam and his captains stout.
Broadside for broadside, half the day,
   But the sturdy enemy still held out ;

Till about four bells in the afternoon
  The English suddenly ceased their fire,
And Van Dam hailed : " Have you struck so soon ?
  Is the score then settled, may I inquire ? "

And the answer came : " No ; we have not struck,
  But our powder is spent ; we can fight no more."
" Ah, that is a matter of evil luck,
  In a case like this," said the Commodore.

Then he stroked his beard and he closed his eyes :
  " 'T were a pity to mar so sweet a fight,
On a beggarly question of supplies.
  Diable ! it spoils one's pleasure quite."

With the thrifty blood of his Holland sire
  A stream of a warmer fluid ran,
From a Norman mother with heart of fire —
  And the mother it is that makes the man.

" To win or to lose," said the blood of France,
  " Were a problem simple as life or death ;
But to win by an enemy's dull mischance ! " —
  He damned the lubbers below his breath.

Then : " Send me your boat aboard," he cried,
  " If you will not strike and you cannot fight.

Pity your stubborn bulldog pride
  Should bark so loud, with so small a bite ! ''

The Admiral came in his gig of state ;
  A captain by right of heritage,
Favor had made him all but great,
  And Nature had never marred the page.

Dutchman all was the Commodore
  At once when he saw his wondrous guest,
Marveling much and marveling more
  As he listed the visitor's request.

Never was such proposal made
  To sailor before, on land or sea :
'' 'T was awkward to dabble in vulgar trade ;
  But have you some powder to sell to me ? ''

Dutch diplomacy struggled hard,
  But Gallic chivalry won the day.
The sale was made and the bill was paid,
  And the guns went back to their pleasant play.

Ill had it gone with the Commodore,
  Had pluck or fortune deceived him then ;
But he fought as he never fought before,
  And he brought his investment back again.

The great States-General, solemn folk,
  When old Van Dam came home next day,
With his prizes in tow, forgave the joke,
  Or never perceived it — who can say?

Half the race of life is over, and the breeze is well
abaft.
Do we lead or do we follow? — naught it matters
to us now.
All the joy was in the battle of the windward-run-
ning craft,
In the squall against the topsail, in the wave before the prow.

Oh, the consorts who were with us in the opening
of the race!
Ah, the daring shallops foundered as we sailed
into the wind !
Oh, the sweet and foolish passions when the sun
was in our face,
And we left the laggard Prudence league on
league away behind !

Then a friend was had for loving, and we loved
without a thought ;
We saw our hearts were naked, and we shamed
not of the truth.

28

But the sober fruit of knowledge aye in bitterness
    is bought,
And the flaming sword forever bars the Eden
    gate of youth.

JACK CREAMER

A TRUE STORY OF 1812

THE boarding nettings are triced for fight ;
Pike and cutlass are shining bright ;
The boatswain's whistle pipes loud and shrill ;
Gunner and topman work with a will ;
Rough old sailor and reefer trim
Jest as they stand by the cannon grim ;
There 's a fighting glint in Decatur's eye,
And brave Old Glory floats out on high.

But many a heart beats fast below
The laughing lips as they near the foe ;
For the pluckiest knows, though no man quails,
That the breath of death is filling the sails.
Only one little face is wan ;
Only one childish mouth is drawn ;
One little heart is sad and sore
To the watchful eye of the Commodore.
Little Jack Creamer, ten years old,
In no purser's book or watch enrolled,

Must mope or skulk while his shipmates fight, —
No wonder his little face is white !

"Why, Jack, old man, so blue and sad ?
Afraid of the music?" The face of the lad
With mingled shame and anger burns.
Quick to the Commodore he turns :
"I 'm not a coward, but I think if you —
Excuse me, Capt'n, I mean if you knew
(I s'pose it 's because I 'm young and small)
I 'm not on the books!   I 'm no one at all !
And as soon as this fighting work is done
And we get our prize-money, every one
Has his share of the plunder — *I* get none."

"And you 're sure we shall take her?"   "Sure?
      Why, sir,
She 's only a blessed Britisher!
We 'll take her easy enough, I bet ;
But glory 's all that I 'm going to get ! "

"Glory!   I doubt if I get more,
If I get so much," said the Commodore ;
" But faith goes far in the race for fame,
And down on the books shall go your name."

Bravely the little seaman stood
To his post while the scuppers ran with blood,

While grizzled veterans looked and smiled
And gathered new courage from the child;
Till the enemy, crippled in pride and might,
Struck his crimson flag and gave up the fight.
Then little Jack Creamer stood once more
Face to face with the Commodore.

"You have got your glory," he said, "my lad,
And money to make your sweetheart glad.
Now, who may she be?"   "My mother, sir;
I want you to send the half to her."
"And the rest?"   Jack blushed and hung his head;
"I 'll buy some schoolin' with that," he said.

Decatur laughed; then in graver mood:
"The first is the better, but both are good.
Your mother shall never know want while I
Have a ship to sail, or a flag to fly;
And schooling you 'll have till all is blue,
But little the lubbers can teach to you."

Midshipman Creamer's story is told —
They did such things in the days of old,
When faith and courage won sure reward,
And the quarter-deck was not triply barred,
To the forecastle hero; for men were men,
And the Nation was close to its Maker then.

THE FLAG

I NEVER have got the bearings quite,
  Though I 've followed the course for many a
    year,
If he was crazy, clean outright,
  Or only what you might say was "queer."

He was just a simple sailor man.
  I mind it as well as yisterday,
When we messed aboard of the old Cyane.
  Lord! how the time does slip away!
That was five and thirty year ago,
  And I never expect such times again,
For sailors was n't afraid to stow
  Themselves on a Yankee vessel then.
He was only a sort of bosun's mate,
  But every inch of him taut and trim;
Stars and anchors and togs of state
  Tailors don't build for the like of him.
He flew a no-account sort of name,

A reg'lar fo'cas'le " Jim " or " Jack,"
With a plain " McGinnis " abaft the same,
　Giner'ly reefed to simple " Mack."
Mack, we allowed, was sorter queer, —
　Ballast or compass was n't right.
Till he licked four Juicers one day, a fear
　Prevailed that he had n't larned to fight.
But I reckon the Captain knowed his man,
　When he put the flag in his hand the day
That we went ashore from the old Cyane,
　On a madman's cruise for Darien Bay.

Forty days in the wilderness
　We toiled and suffered and starved with Strain,
Losing the number of many a mess
　In the Devil's swamps of the Spanish Main.
All of us starved, and many died.
　One laid down, in his dull despair ;
His stronger messmate went to his side —
　We left them both in the jungle there.
It was hard to part with shipmates so ;
　But standing by would have done no good.
We heard them moaning all day, so slow
　We dragged along through the weary wood.
McGinnis, he suffered the worst of all ;
　Not that he ever piped his eye
Or would n't have answered to the call

If they 'd sounded it for " All hands to die."
I guess 't would have sounded for him before,
   But the grit inside of him kept him strong,
Till we met relief on the river shore ;
   And we all broke down when it came along.

All but McGinnis.   Gaunt and tall,
   Touching his hat, and standing square :
" Captain, the Flag." . . . And that was all ;
   He just keeled over and foundered there.
" The Flag ? "   We thought he had lost his head —
   It might n't be much to lose at best —
Till we came, by and by, to dig his bed,
   And we found it folded around his breast.
He laid so calm and smiling there,
   With the flag wrapped tight about his heart ;
Maybe he saw his course all fair,
   Only — *we* could n't read the chart.

SIR HUGO'S CHOICE

IT is better to die, since death comes surely,
  In the full noontide of an honored name,
Than to lie at the end of years obscurely,
  A handful of dust in a shroud of shame.

.   .   .   .

Sir Hugo lived in the ages golden,
  Warder of Aisne and Picardy ;
He lived and died, and his deeds are told in
  The Book immortal of Chivalric :

How he won the love of a prince's daughter —
  A poor knight he with a stainless sword —
Whereat Count Rolf, who had vainly sought her,
  Swore death should sit at the bridal board.

"A braggart's threat, for a brave man's scorn-
      ing !"
  And Hugo laughed at his rival's ire,
But couriers twain, on the bridal morning,
  To his castle gate came with tidings dire.

The first a-faint and with armor riven :
 " In peril sore have I left thy bride, —
False Rolf waylaid us.   For love and Heaven!
 Sir Hugo, quick to the rescue ride ! "

Stout Hugo muttered a word unholy ;
 He sprang to horse and he flashed his brand,
But a hand was laid on his bridle slowly,
 And a herald spoke : " By the king's command

"This to Picardy's trusty warder : —
 France calls first for his loyal sword,
The Flemish spears are across the border,
 And all is lost if they win the ford."

Sir Hugo paused, and his face was ashen,
 His white lips trembled in silent prayer —
God's pity soften the spirit's passion
 When the crucifixion of Love is there !

What need to tell of the message spoken ?
 Of the hand that shook as he poised his lance ?
And the look that told of his brave heart broken,
 As he bade them follow, " For God and France ! "

On Cambray's field next morn they found him,
 'Mid a mighty swath of foemen dead ;

Her snow-white scarf he had bound around him
  With his loyal blood was baptizèd red.

It is all writ down in the book of glory,
  On crimson pages of blood and strife,
With scanty thought for the simple story
  Of duty dearer than love or life.

Only a note obscure, appended
  By warrior scribe or monk perchance,
Saith : "The good knight's ladye was sore offended
  That he would not die for her but France."

Did the ladye live to lament her lover ?
  Or did roystering Rolf prove a better mate ?
I have searched the records over and over,
  But naught discover to tell her fate.

And I read the moral — A brave endeavor
  To do thy duty, whate'er its worth,
Is better than life with love forever —
  And love is the sweetest thing on earth.

GETTYSBURG

THERE was no union in the land,
  Though wise men labored long
With links of clay and ropes of sand
  To bind the right and wrong.

There was no temper in the blade
  That once could cleave a chain;
Its edge was dull with touch of trade
  And clogged with rust of gain.

The sand and clay must shrink away
  Before the lava tide:
By blows and blood and fire assay
  The metal must be tried.

Here sledge and anvil met, and when
  The furnace fiercest roared,
God's undiscerning workingmen
  Reforged His people's sword.

Enough for them to ask and know
The moment's duty clear —
The bayonets flashed it there below,
The guns proclaimed it here :

To do and dare, and die at need,
But while life lasts, to fight —
For right or wrong a simple creed,
But simplest for the right.

They faltered not who stood that day
And held this post of dread ;
Nor cowards they who wore the gray
Until the gray was red.

For every wreath the victor wears
The vanquished half may claim ;
And every monument declares
A common pride and fame.

We raise no altar stones to Hate,
Who never bowed to Fear :
No province crouches at our gate,
To shame our triumph here.

Here standing by a dead wrong's grave
The blindest now may see,

The blow that liberates the slave
But sets the master free!

When ills beset the nation's life
Too dangerous to bear,
The sword must be the surgeon's knife,
Too merciful to spare.

O Soldier of our common land,
'T is thine to bear that blade
Loose in the sheath, or firm in hand,
But ever unafraid.

When foreign foes assail our right,
One nation trusts to thee —·
To wield it well in worthy fight —
The sword of Meade and Lee!

THE MEN OF THE ALAMO

To Houston at Gonzales town, ride, Ranger, for
    your life,
Nor stop to say good-by to-day to home, or child,
    or wife;
But pass the word from ranch to ranch, to every
    Texan sword,
That fifty hundred Mexicans have crossed the
    Nueces ford,
With Castrillon and perjured Cos, Sesmá and
    Almonté,
And Santa Anna ravenous for vengeance and for
    prey!
They smite the land with fire and sword; the
    grass shall never grow
Where northward sweeps that locust horde on San
    Antonio!

Now who will bar the foeman's path, to gain a
    breathing space,
Till Houston and his scattered men shall meet him
    face to face?

Who holds his life as less than naught when home
    and honor call,
And counts the guerdon full and fair for liberty to
    fall?
Oh, who but Barrett Travis, the bravest of them
    all!
With seven score of riflemen to play the rancher's
    game,
And feed a counter-fire to halt the sweeping prairie
    flame ;
For Bowie of the broken blade is there to cheer
    them on,
With Evans of Concepcion, who conquered Castril-
    lon,
And o'er their heads the Lone Star flag defiant
    floats on high,
And no man thinks of yielding, and no man fears
    to die.

But ere the siege is held a week a cry is heard
    without,
A clash of arms, a rifle peal, the Ranger's ringing
    shout,
And two-and-thirty beardless boys have bravely
    hewed their way
To die with Travis if they must, to conquer if they
    may.

Was ever bravery so cheap in Glory's mart before
In all the days of chivalry, in all the deeds of war?

But once again the foemen gaze in wonderment and
    fear
To see a stranger break their lines and hear the
    Texans cheer.
God! how they cheered to welcome him, those
    spent and starving men!
For Davy Crockett by their side was worth an
    army then.
The wounded ones forgot their wounds; the dying
    drew a breath
To hail the king of border men, then turned to
    laugh at death.
For all knew Davy Crockett, blithe and generous
    as bold,
And strong and rugged as the quartz that hides its
    heart of gold.
His simple creed for word or deed true as the bul-
    let sped,
And rung the target straight: "Be sure you 're
    right, then go ahead!"

And were they right who fought the fight for Texas
    by his side?
They questioned not; they faltered not; they only
    fought and died.

Who hath an enemy like these, God's mercy slay
    him straight ! —
A thousand Mexicans lay dead outside the convent
    gate,
And half a thousand more must die before the for-
    tress falls,
And still the tide of war beats high around the
    leaguered walls.

At last the bloody breach is won ; the weakened
    lines give way ;
The wolves are swarming in the court ; the lions
    stand at bay.
The leader meets them at the breach, and wins the
    soldier's prize ;
A foeman's bosom sheathes his sword when gallant
    Travis dies.
Now let the victor feast at will until his crest be
    red —
We may not know what raptures fill the vulture
    with the dead.
Let Santa Anna's valiant sword right bravely hew
    and hack
The senseless corse ; its hands are cold ; they will
    not strike him back.
Let Bowie die, but 'ware the hand that wields his
    deadly knife ;

Four went to slay, and one comes back, so dear he
    sells his life.
And last of all let Crockett fall, too proud to sue
    for grace,
So grand in death the butcher dared not look upon
    his face.

.   .   .   .

But far on San Jacinto's field the Texan toils are
    set,
And Alamo's dread memory the Texan steel shall
    whet.
And Fame shall tell their deeds who fell till all the
    years be run.
"Thermopylæ left one alive — the Alamo left
    none."

JOHN BOYLE O'REILLY

August 10, 1890

HAVE thy people climbed to Nebo?
　Is the Promised Land in sight,
And the pleasant fields of Canaan
　Radiant in the morning light?

Strike the harp, and sound the timbrel,
　For the weary night is past,
For their wanderings are over,
　And the day hath come at last.

Lift on high the little children;
　Lead the elders forth to see;
Let the maidens sing in gladness
　Of the joy that is to be.

Now for them the bulwarks totter,
　Now for them the Jordan dries, —
But our Chief is dead on Phasga;
　In the stranger land he lies.

Wonder not if we be silent ;
  Chide not if our eyes be dim ;
We are mourning for our Prophet —
  Israel hath no more like him !

THE LAST OF THE DRUIDS

CONAL, last of the Druids, stood by the ruined
    shrine,
And the ashes were cold on the altar and bitter and
    gray as brine ;
The sacred grove was deserted, and impious hands
    had raised
The mystic sign of the stranger where the holy fires
    had blazed.
He went to the home of his father, and a stranger
    bade him in
Who knew not the face of Conal nor came of his
    father's kin.

For the years were many and changeful since the
    Druid went afar
From the peaceful land of Ierne to the stormy fields
    of war.
He had battled with Pict and Briton, Norseman
    and Hun and Gaul,
When Dathi's glorious banner waved on the Alpine
    wall.

And now he was old, and weary of the splendid
    joy of strife,
And he longed for the Druid cloister and the even- -
    ing calm of life :
"The gods of the brave will bless me for the foes
    I have slain," he said,
And he turned to the land of Ierne — and they
    told him the gods were dead !

Then he cursed the gods of his fathers, the many
    who fled from one,
And he cursed the priest of the stranger for the
    thing that he had done.
"I will find this priest, I will slay him, — let him
    bide on land or sea,
Though a thousand swords defend him — and the
    gods shall be shamed by me !"

He went to the Court of Tara where the king had
    housed the priest ;
He found him not at the palace, he found him not
    at the feast ;
But down in a lowly hovel, where a man with the
    Black Death lay,
They told him, " The good priest, Patrick, watches
    by night and day ;
For the man he serves was his foeman in the days
    of his power and pride,

But the pride and the power have left him, and the
    love of his friends has died ;
Kith or kin has he none — only one son, gone
    wild —
And the Black Death's hand, Christ save us ! would
    part the mother and child.
The boldest soldier in Erin, I warrant ye, would
    not dare
To watch with old Conn the Druid, in the deadly
    pest-house there."

Never a word said Conal, but his face was set and
    gray,
As he strode to the lonely cabin where the dying
    Druid lay.
He knelt by the humble pallet, and the air was
    thick with death,
But the lips of the stricken father smiled with his
    dying breath,
And his feeble hand was lifted to bless with the
    Christian's sign
The wayward son of his bosom — the last of the
    Druid line.

Then the sinful wrath of Conal passed like a mist
    away,
And he kissed the hem of the garment of the man
    he had sworn to slay.

WASHINGTON

God wills no man a slave.   The man most meek,
Who saw Him face to face on Horeb's peak,
Had slain a tyrant for a bondman's wrong,
And met his Lord with sinless soul and strong.
But when, years after, overfraught with care,
His feet once trod doubt's pathway to despair,
For that one treason lapse, the guiding hand
That led so far now barred the promised land.
God makes no man a slave, no doubter free;
Abiding faith alone wins liberty.

No angel led our Chieftain's steps aright;
No pilot cloud by day, no flame by night;
No plague nor portent spake to foe or friend;
No doubt assailed him, faithful to the end.

Weaklings there were, as in the tribes of old,
Who craved for fleshpots, worshiped calves of
        gold,
Murmured that right should harder be than wrong,
And freedom's narrow road so steep and long;

But he who ne'er on Sinai's summit trod,
Still walked the highest heights and spake with
    God ;
Saw with anointed eyes no promised land
By petty bounds or pettier cycles spanned,
Its people curbed and broken to the ring,
Packed with a caste and saddled with a king—
But freedom's heritage and training school,
Where man unruled should learn to wisely rule,
Till sun and moon should see at Ajalon
Kings' heads in dust and freemen's feet thereon.

His work well done, the leader stepped aside,
Spurning a crown with more than kingly pride,
Content to wear the higher crown of worth,
While time endures, First Citizen of earth.

THE LAY BROTHER'S STORY

THAT is his grave, and this is mine —
The Father was good to me so old,
Though I spake no word and I made no sign,
Nor ever nourished a hope so bold
As to dream that my dust by his might lie,
Who was saint on earth and is saint on high.

Forty years together we wrought,
And not one look from him to tell
That his mind went back for a fleeting thought
To the life we both had known so well.
For he had been here two years before
I left the world and curbed my tongue,
And I knew him well in the days of yore
When I was not old and he was young.

Never a sign through all the years
Till yesterday when his summons came,
And I saw him smile through a veil of tears,
And he took my hand and he called my name:

(For one hour of life, ere it fades away,
To the dying Trappist is kindly given,
That his soul may see, when its sins are shriven,
How as death to life, and as night to day,
Are the joys of earth to the Joy of Heaven !)

Then the Angel of Memory rolled the stone
Back from the sepulchre of years,
Till the forty winters of monotone
And the forty summers our cells had known
Were gone, and we two were grenadiers —
Grenadiers of the Grande Armée,
Side by side on that woful day
At Kowno Bridge with the godlike Ney,
Facing ten thousand Cossack spears.
I saw him fall as they pressed us back,
Inch by inch, to the further shore ;
Then a mist of blood hid the battle wrack,
And I prayed to awaken nevermore.
But God's great mercy denied the boon
And gave me life and some deeds to do,
Till the end that came so sore and soon
In shame and sorrow and Waterloo.
Small loss was it then to leave the earth
That held no longer or hope or dread ;
But great the reward beyond my worth,
For I found him here I had mourned for dead.

I marveled oft if he never thought
Of France and glory and dreams so dear
To our dear dead youth — ah! I forgot
The saint had been man — and a grenadier!

He held my hand, and the long desire
Spake through his eyes and the glaze of death;
Something was, too, of the old-time fire
Men feel when they taste the battle-breath.
And something more of the love so strong
No years could weaken, no reason chill,
For the Chief we followed through right or wrong,
As the planets swing to the great Sun's will.

God will not love him less, I know,
For the love that gnawed at his silent breast
Through years of speechless doubt and woe,
For Himself hath said that love is best,
And all that he asked I freely told,
And would tell again though I died therefor —
"Tell me," he said, "my comrade old,
Tell me about my Emperor!"

WHITTIER

A law well kept in Otaheite saith:
" Speak not the Monarch's name on pain of death!"

HIGH on his throne majestic Wrong
　　Triumphant sate, and all in awe
Paid homage due — amid the throng
　　Was none so supple-kneed as Law.

The patriot at the shrine of Self
　　With hardly more devotion bowed,
The trader eager-eyed for pelf,
　　The pulpit politician loud,

And all the mob of caste and class,
　　Before the throne with tribute drew
And groveled low, as loth to pass ;
　　But no man spake the name *taboo*,

Till Freedom's poet came and sung,
　　And slaves of Slavery in shame
No longer held the servile tongue —
　　For all men spake the tyrant's name.

57

NEED we tell the stirring story of the builders of
the Town
Where the record of their glory every stone hath
written down ?

Do we look beyond the ripeness, to the sapling or
the root ?
Nay, we know the tree is healthy — we have tasted
of the fruit.

Fair and stately is the city, from the lowly hamlet
grown ;
But its strength is ruled and measured by the hidden corner-stone.

Not in darkness, but in wisdom, wrought the pre-
scient pioneers,
Hewing pathways, building bridges, for the march-
ing of the years,

For the glorious procession that their eyes might
    never see
Of the serried ages moving to the light of Liberty ;

Moving slowly, footsore, weary, for the road is dark
    and long,
Every passage barred by Power, every hilltop held
    by Wrong ;

Till the dawn of Freedom breaketh, with the prom-
    ised land in view,
Where the simple many toil not for the strong and
    cunning few,

Where the worker knows no master, and the thinker
    takes no heed
Of the morrow lest he perish in the selfish game of
    greed.

Naught the Fathers recked of hardships, naught
    of triumphs sorely won ;
They but saw the day's endeavor and the duty to
    be done.

For they said : " The sum we know not, but God
    keeps the score in sight ;
Every cipher makes it tenfold, if you place it to the
    right."

Who hath faith may move a mountain.   Aye, for
 faith shall move the man,
And the strong arm of the righteous carry out the
 heavenly plan.

So in sacrifice and travail, as a coral island grows,
With the builders for its ramparts, line by line the
 structure rose.

Not on perishable columns be their faithful names
 enrolled ;
Not in fleeting song or story be their valiant actions
 told.

But by sons who stand for honor, in the council, on
 the field ;
By unspotted civic virtue, Freedom's sword and
 spear and shield ;

By the simple faith and courage left in heritage and
 trust, —
Shall the City hold its charter, when the parchment
 turns to dust !

NATURE THE FALSE GODDESS

THE vilest work of vilest man,
  The cup that drugs, the sword that slays,
The purchased kiss of courtesan,
  The lying tongue of blame or praise,

The cobra's fang, the tiger's spring,
  The python's murderous embrace —
The wrath of any living thing —
  A man may fear but bravely face.

But thou, cold Mother, knowest naught
  Of love, or hate, or joy, or woe ;
Thy bounties come to man unsought,
  Thy curses fall on friend and foe.

Thou bearest balm upon thy breath,
  Or sowest poison in the air ;
And if man reapeth life or death,
  Thou dost not know, thou dost not care.

Thou art God's instrument of fate,
  Obedient, mighty, soulless, blind,
No demon to propitiate,
  No deity in love enshrined.

Let him who turns from God away
  To Bel or Moloch bend the knee,
Defile his soul to wood or clay,
  Or thrill with Voudoo's ecstasy,

Seek any fetich undivine,
  Be any superstition's thrall —
From Heaven or Hell will come a sign,
  But thou alone art deaf to all.

RECANTATION

IT is not wisdom to be over-wise :
At twenty, one knows all ; at thirty, less ;
Happy if even then his blindness he may guess,
Ere forty open his conceited eyes
To their own blankness, with severe surprise, —
Thrice happy if his folly he confess,
Who thought to find his perfect happiness
In tepid Friendship's unpoetic guise.

A timid sailor of the temperate zone,
I said : " Joy dwells not North, nor East, nor West,
Nor anywhere save in the sea-ways known
Where consort souls find harmony and rest " —
Till sudden Southward was my shallop blown,
And then, at last, I knew that Love was best.

A SAILOR'S YARN

THIS is the tale that was told to me
  By a battered and shattered son of the sea, —
To me and my messmate, Silas Green,
  When I was a guileless young marine.

'T was the good ship Gyascutus,
  All in the China seas,
With the wind a-lee and the capstan free
  To catch the summer breeze.

'T was Captain Porgie on the deck,
  To his mate in the mizzen hatch,
While the boatswain bold, in the forward hold,
  Was winding his larboard watch.

"Oh, how does our good ship head to-night?
  How heads our gallant craft?"
"Oh, she heads to the E. S. W. by N.,
  And the binnacle lies abaft!"

" Oh, what does the quadrant indicate,
　　And how does the sextant stand?"
" Oh, the sextant's down to the freezing point,
　　And the quadrant's lost a hand!"

" Oh, and if the quadrant has lost a hand
　　And the sextant falls so low,
　It's our bodies and bones to Davy Jones
　　This night are bound to go!

" Oh, fly aloft to the garboard strake!
　　And reef the spanker boom;
　Bend a studding-sail on the martingale,
　　To give her weather room.

" O boatswain, down in the for'ard hold,
　　What water do you find?"
" Four foot and a half by the royal gaff
　　And rather more behind!"

" O sailors, collar your marline spikes
　　And each belaying-pin;
　Come, stir your stumps and spike the pumps,
　　Or more will be coming in!"

They stirred their stumps, they spiked the pumps,
　　They spliced the mizzen brace;

Aloft and alow they worked, but oh!
The water gained apace.

They bored a hole above the keel
To let the water out;
But, strange to say, to their dismay,
The water in did spout.

Then up spoke the Cook of our gallant ship,
And he was a lubber brave:
" I have several wives in various ports,
And my life I 'd orter save."

Then up spoke the Captain of Marines,
Who dearly loved his prog:
" It 's awful to die, and it 's worse to be dry,
And I move we pipes to grog."

Oh, then 't was the noble second mate
What filled them all with awe;
The second mate, as bad men hate,
And cruel skippers jaw.

He took the anchor on his back
And leaped into the main;
Through foam and spray he clove his way,
And sunk and rose again!

Through foam and spray, a league away
  The anchor stout he bore ;
Till, safe at last, he made it fast
  And warped the ship ashore !

'T ain't much of a job to talk about,
  But a ticklish thing to see,
And suth'in to do, if I say it, too,
  For that second mate was me !

Such was the tale that was told to me
By that modest and truthful son of the sea ;
And I envy the life of a second mate,
Though captains curse him and sailors hate,
For he ain't like some of the swabs I 've seen,
As would go and lie to a poor marine.

HOPE

THE star you seem to see, love,
  With eyes more bright and clear,
All dark and dead may be, love,
  This many a hundred year.

But though its fires may never
  Send forth another ray,
That beam through space forever
  Shall wing its shining way.

So, spite of saints and sages
  And maxims manifold,
Love lives through all the ages,
  Though hope be dead and cold.

68

www.ingramcontent.com/pod-product-compliance
Lightning Source LLC
Chambersburg PA
CBHW030015030726
47499CB00008B/3007